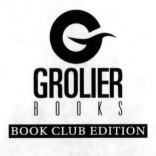

The Wubbulous world of Dr. Seuss™

The Gink

by **Tish Rabe**
adapted from a script by **Belinda Ward**
illustrated by **Joe Ewers**

Random House/Jim Henson Productions

The Dorfmans are shopping.
They're hoping to get

Eliza a present,
and she wants a pet.

Her parents are hoping
she won't even think
of choosing the one pet she can't have . . .

. . . the Gink!

What's a Gink?

It's a bit like a gunk.
And a lot like a skink
that *gooblaatts* day and night
and sprays spots of pink ink.

Eliza had seen every pet in the store.
Mr. Puttmutter cried,
"There just aren't any more."

"I know what we'll buy,"
said the girl with a wink.
"The one pet I want
to take home is—the Gink!"

The store owner smiled.
"With your Gink you will need
a videotape
and these twelve books to read!"

So the Dorfmans went home.
Then they heard a *gooblatt!*

"The tape," cried Eliza,
"tells the meaning of that!"

They turned on the tape
and they heard a voice say:
"This is Horton the Elephant
coming your way.

"Did your Gink *gooblatt?*
You must feed him, please.
Give him Gloopa fruit that
only grows in South Geeze."

"Gloopa fruit!" cried Eliza.
"I'll find some today.

I am off to South Geeze.
I'll be back right away."

When Eliza got back
she fed her poor Gink.

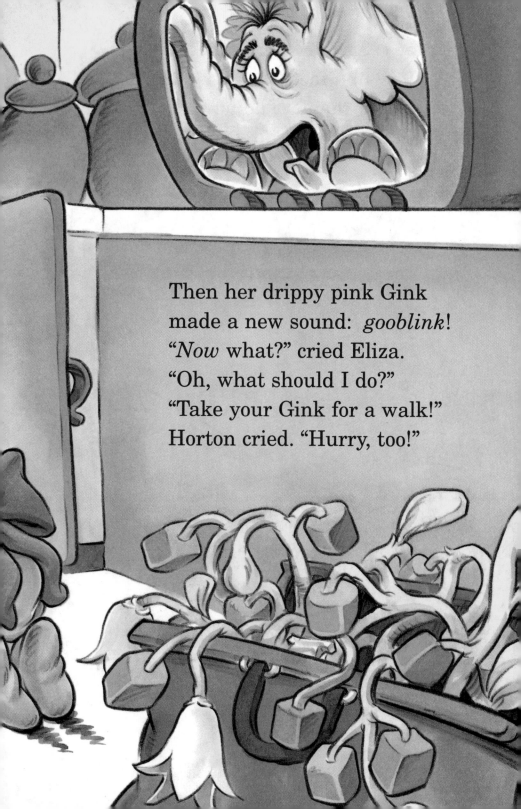

Then her drippy pink Gink
made a new sound: *gooblink!*
"*Now* what?" cried Eliza.
"Oh, what should I do?"
"Take your Gink for a walk!"
Horton cried. "Hurry, too!"

So they ran to the park
and met Ronald Q. Clark,
a ranger who never
stays out after dark.

Before Ronald knew it,
he found himself stuck
to the Gink, who was covered
with ick-sticky guck!

So she un-gucked her Gink.
But he started to stink!

"I am taking you back!
Quick as a wink!"

Gooblett! cried her Gink,
and Eliza just knew
that the Gink really loved her,
and she loved him, too.

But by morning her Gink,
was feeling quite blue.

So she called the Pet Hotline.
They said, "Lucky you!
Your Gink will be seen
by not one doc—but two!"

"This Gink," said the doctors,
"is lonely. So please
take him back to his home
in far-off South Geeze!"

Take her
Gink home?
She just couldn't
do *that!*

"We'll act just like Ginks.
We'll say *gooblink* and *gooblatt*."
The neighbors complained
about all the *gooblinking*.
"Just what," they wondered,
"can the Dorfmans be thinking?"

The long weeks went by
and one day the Gink sighed.
"My Gink," said Eliza,
"please know that we tried.

I see now that keeping you
with me was wrong.
So I'm taking you home,
back where you belong."

Once in South Geeze, she said,
"Stick to your mother.
Go play with your brother.
Stay close to each other.

I'll write to you often,
and visit you soon.
Every Tuesday and Thursday,
and the whole month of June."

Next day from the pet store
she got a surprise.
A pretty pink kitten
with green-and-blue eyes!

But the first time she gave
her new kitten a pat,
it opened its mouth
and out came a . . .